Amy Schwartz and Leonard S. Marcus

Oscar

The Big Adventure of a Little Sock Monkey

Illustrated by Amy Schwartz

KATHERINE TEGEN BOOKS
An Imprint of HarperCollinsPublishers

Susie Green, a girl with a happy smile, lived in a big apartment house in the big city. Oscar, a little brown sock monkey, lived on Susie Green's bed. And Cottontail, a fat white rabbit, lived in a wire cage on the bedroom floor.

They were all best friends.

Now, Susie was a fine girl, but a bit forgetful. Oscar did a good job of looking after her.

He kept track of Susie's barrettes.

He freshened Cottontail's water when Susie forgot.

And he pulled up her blankets at night.

Oscar's life was a happy though a quiet one.
But one day he had an adventure he would never forget.
It all began the morning of the school pet show. Susie
and Cottontail had left early. Oscar was just waking from
a lovely dream when he felt something sharp poking his
bottom. It was the key to Cottontail's cage!

Susie had forgotten the key. How could Susie win a blue ribbon at the pet show if she couldn't get Cottontail out of the cage?

Oscar slipped the silver key and ribbon over his head. He knew what needed to be done.

He knew that Susie and Cottontail were at Washington School at the corner of 81st and Second. But where was that?

Oscar found a map in the kitchen drawer and charted his route.

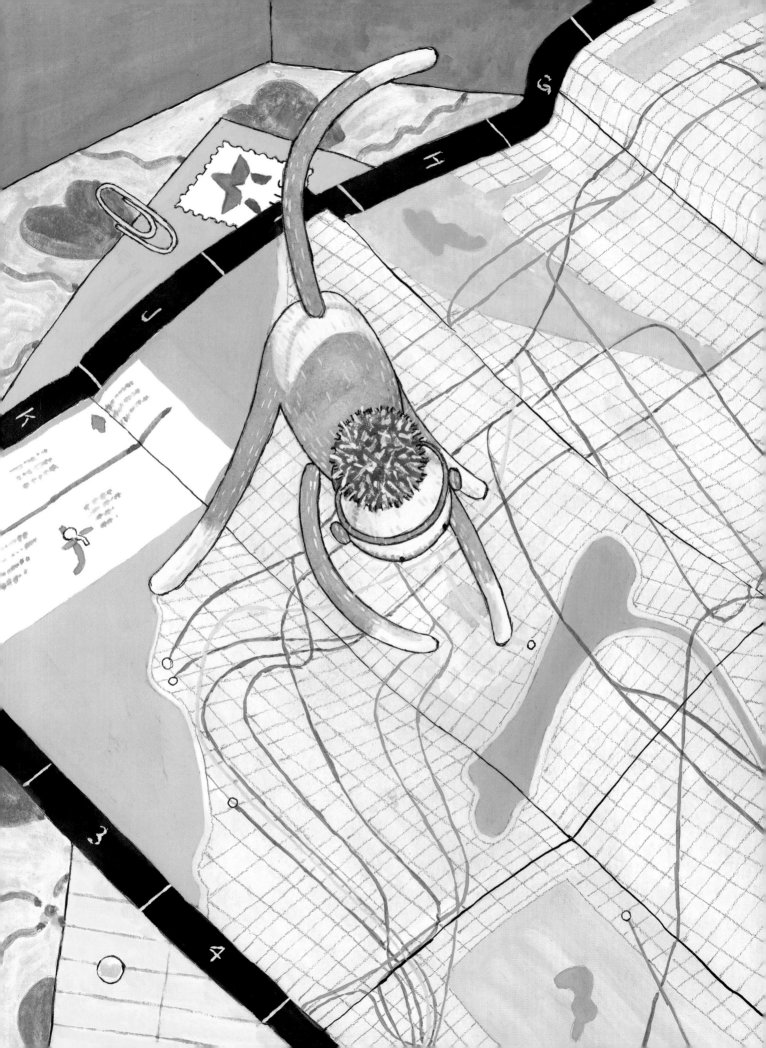

Oscar had never been out on his own before. He straightened his pom-pom and slipped out the door. It was a quick ride to the lobby. After a few turns in the revolving door and a breath of city air, Oscar headed down the subway steps.

Suddenly, there on
the platform was music.
The tune was catchy.
Oscar had to dance.

When the No. 4 train arrived, Oscar scurried aboard and found a seat. At Lincoln Square, a huge rubber plant boarded the train. Oscar leaned forward to get a closer look and . . .

. . . there he was, knee-deep in topsoil.

For one dark moment, it seemed as though Oscar's journey had ended in a pot of dirt. But Oscar decided to make the best of things and, with a mighty effort, pulled himself free. He was just imagining himself on a desert island . . .

. . . when Oscar realized the pot was getting off the train.

"Eighty-sixth and Second! Watch the doors!" the speaker blared.

What luck! It was Oscar's stop, too. Oscar prepared to exit.

Unfortunately, he exited into a passing shopping bag filled with white boxes tied with red string. Oscar decided to investigate.

"Cupcakes! My favorite!" Oscar exclaimed. He meant only to take a bite, but they were so fresh, they were so good, and they were chocolate.

Somehow it was ten blocks
before Oscar slipped from the
bag. Brushing a few crumbs from
his pom-pom, Oscar headed
downtown.

When he caught sight of
Washington School, Oscar began
to jog.

Splat! A stream of water hit Oscar.
Water was flying everywhere. It was all
Oscar could do to keep his pom-pom dry and
his wits about him.

But it wasn't raining. A giant fourth grader was
squirting a water pistol. He was shooting at a curly-haired
boy half his size holding a black-and-white puppy.

Oscar leapt into action. He jumped on the bully's big
toe and danced a jig.

"What the . . ." the bully screamed.

The little boy scrambled to safety through the school doors.

"You're coming with me!" the bully said as he stuffed
Oscar into his jacket pocket and snapped it shut.

It was dark inside the pocket, and clammy. Oscar was
stuck to something.

He sniffed. Butterscotch!
Oscar grabbed a pencil and
yanked himself clear.

He almost lost his grip when a
huge voice boomed, "Attention,
Mrs. Smith's second-grade class!
Please report to the auditorium.
The pet show has begun!"

"Susie, hold on!" Oscar
called. "I'm on my way!"

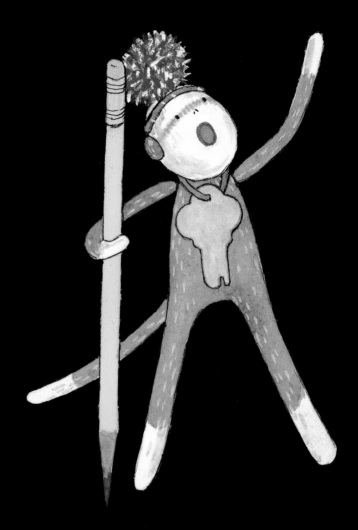

Oscar began to poke the
pencil along the bottom of the
pocket.
"Eureka!"
There was a sliver of light.
With all his strength, Oscar
dug at the cloth.

All at once, the pocket split wide open. As Oscar tumbled head over heels, his tail sprung into action and he dangled from a jacket cord. He looked about wildly.

What luck! The curly-haired boy with his black-and-white puppy were coming around the corner with his class.

The puppy's eyes met Oscar's. Quick as a wink, the pup pulled up within inches of Oscar's pom-pom, and Oscar jumped.

Oscar and the puppy trotted quickly into the auditorium.

Susie was just climbing the steps to the stage.

"Susie Green will now share with us," the principal announced.

Oscar thanked the puppy, dismounted, and scurried onstage. He ran up the curtains onto the catwalk high above. He pulled the silver key and ribbon off over his head and took aim.

It was a perfect shot.

"Yes!" He chuckled softly as the key fell
neatly into Susie's front pocket.

Susie fished the silver key out of her pocket and
unlocked Cottontail's cage.

"This is my rabbit, Cottontail," she said. "She lives in
my room with my monkey, Oscar. We are all best friends."

Everybody clapped.

Susie smiled her happy smile.

And Oscar, one ounce of cotton happiness, began to
plan his way home.

For Jacob

Oscar: The Big Adventure of a Little Sock Monkey
Text copyright © 2006 by Amy Schwartz and Leonard S. Marcus
Illustrations copyright © 2006 by Amy Schwartz
Manufactured in China.
For information address HarperCollins Children's Books,
a division of HarperCollins Publishers,
1350 Avenue of the Americas, New York, NY 10019.
www.harperchildrens.com

Library of Congress Cataloging-in-Publication Data

Schwartz, Amy.
  Oscar : the big adventure of a little sock monkey / story by Amy Schwartz and Leonard Marcus ; illustrated by Amy Schwartz.—
1st ed.
      p.   cm.
  Summary: A sock monkey named Oscar saves the day for his little girl at the school pet show.
  ISBN-13: 978-0-06-072622-5 (trade bdg.)
  ISBN-10: 0-06-072622-9 (trade bdg.)
  ISBN-13: 978-0-06-072623-2 (lib. bdg.)
  ISBN-10: 0-06-072623-7 (lib. bdg.)
  [1. Toys—Fiction. 2. Rabbits—Fiction. 3. Schools—Fiction. 4. Pet shows—Fiction.] I. Marcus, Leonard S., 1950- II. Title.
PZ7.S406Osc 2006   2005015631
[E]—dc22   CIP
                                                                                                                              AC

Typography by Jeanne L. Hogle
1 2 3 4 5 6 7 8 9 10
❖
First Edition